Birthday Girl

AN ORIGINAL SCREENPLAY BY

TOM BUTTERWORTH
and
JEZ BUTTERWORTH

Birthday Girl

**talk
miramax
books**

HYPERION

New York

Portobello Pictures copyright © 2001

ISBN 0-7868-8588-2

All rights reserved. No part of this book may be used or reproduced in any manner whatsoever without the written permission of the publisher. Printed in the United States of America. For information address: Hyperion, 77 West 66 Street, New York, New York, 10023-6298

Birthday Girl

VOICE-OVER
nadia in russian with subtitles

SUBTITLE

When I was a little girl, my father gave me his
binoculars. He said: "With these you will find the
one you love."

fade in:

*In a Russian summer meadow, a young girl spins around and around.
A simple guitar theme plays as the low sun catches her hair. Around
her neck is a pair of field binoculars, and she runs through the
meadow with them pressed to her face, spying butterflies, birds,
rabbits.*

WOMAN'S VOICE

(Distant)
Nadia . . . Nadia! Na-dia . . . !

The little girl aims the binoculars up, up into the sun.

fade through sun to:

int. john's house. living room. room.

*A blurred face sharpens into focus. This is John Buckingham, about
thirty.*

JOHN

Hello.

He gets up.

blackout. fade up.

He is sitting as before, looking at us.

blackout. fade up.

JOHN (CONT'D)

Running. Reading. Going out. Staying in. The country-side. Films, if they're good.

blackout. fade up.

JOHN (CONT'D)

Intelligent, of course. Kind. Pretty, I suppose. But it's not critical.

blackout. fade up.

JOHN (CONT'D)

Someone you can really talk to. I think communication is key.

We see that John is talking to his PC. It has a small digital camera on the top. We see him through the eye of the Web cam.

JOHN (CONT'D)

I should say that some people on the face of it might

not understand what I'm doing. So why am I doing
this? Why am I doing it?

He stares at the camera.

MUSIC.

*John's fingers in close-up, type JOHN BUCKINGHAM, and his AMEX
number into his PC.*

*On his computer screen: the Web page for FROM RUSSIA WITH LOVE
and a movie montage of Russian women, on computer video, advertising
themselves. They mostly speak in Russian, some speak in English.*

*The women slide on and off the screen, overlap and collide. Close-ups
on mouths and eyes, tight and pixelated. It becomes a wall of image
and sound.*

Finished, he stops, and rests his face on his hands.

He hits SEND.

blackout:

MUSIC.

TITLES: BIRTHDAY GIRL

ext. st. albans. day.

We swoop over lines of houses and back gardens.

fade to:

3

ext. john's garden. day.

John sprints down his lawn, scattering the big black crows eating his garden. He jumps the fence, and across the fields.

ext. john's drive. day.

John watches while two moving men lift a new double bed from the back of a van.

int. john's house. bedroom. day.

John's hands smooth a crisp white sheet over the double mattress. An ant runs across the sheet. John squashes it and picks it carefully off.

int. lounge. day.

Extreme close-up of the computer keyboard with an ant racing across it.

int. kitchen. day.

A lid is pried off a tube of ant powder.

ext. garden. day.

John encircles his house, leaving a thick trail of yellow powder behind him.

int. john's bedroom. night.

John lies in bed—wide awake.

ext. john's close. day.

John leaves the house.

int. john's car. day

John tries to start the car but it falters. Finally he gets it going.

ext. motorway. day.

From above we see John's car join the motorway.

cut to:

ext. airport. sky. day.

The GIGANTIC UNDERSIDE of a Boeing 747 TEARS down the screen.

int. airport escalator. day.

John slides upview, motionless, toward arrivals.

> JOHN (V/O)
> Dear John. My name is Nadia. I am from Moscow,
> Russia.

int. airport arrivals. day.

Last calls for flights leaving for the other side of the world.

Travelers criss-cross and swirl.

> JOHN (V/O)
> I have been studying English for five years.

int. arrivals gate. day.

The arrivals gate slides open and passengers flood through.

> JOHN (V/O)
> I chose your picture because you have both
> shyness and strength, and you have sad but true
> eyes.

John stands among the crowd, as the passengers trundle by.

*We follow one young woman long enough to think this must be
her . . .*

> JOHN (V/O) (CONT'D)
> I do not say I am your true love, but if you are mine,
> I will know it and I will hear your footsteps among
> ten thousand men.

*. . . but it's a false alarm, she's lifted up and spun around by someone
else.*

> JOHN (V/O) (CONT'D)
> I send a whisper across the world, John. Can you
> hear it?

They've all passed. That's that. She wasn't on the flight.

*John wanders away from the gate. He stands around in the swirl
in the middle of the airport. People bustle by. Everyone is going
somewhere.*

Gradually, we get the sense we are being watched.

*A woman stands nearby. She is about twenty, very beautiful, tired, and
laden with luggage.*

> JOHN

Nadia?

She nods.

> JOHN (CONT'D)

I'm John.

They shake hands.

> JOHN (CONT'D)

Welcome.
(pause)
Right.

He points to her luggage.

> JOHN (CONT'D)

Is that everything?

> NADIA

Yes.

They stand there.

int. john's car [moving]. day.

The silence in the car lasts just long enough for John to feel he is breaking it.

> JOHN
>
> It's about forty miles from here. I don't know if you've had a chance to look at a map . . . It's close to London but it's a city in itself. A Roman city.

John glances across.

> JOHN (CONT'D)
>
> I'm having a problem with ants. It's the warmer weather. I can't seem to find the nest.
> *(pause)*
> This is strange, isn't it.

> NADIA
>
> Yes.

> JOHN
>
> I mean . . . "Ants." "I've got a problem with ants." Honestly.

He shakes his head. Nadia lights up a cigarette and looks out of the window.

> JOHN (CONT'D)
>
> Right. So. You're a smoker.
> *(pause)*
> I thought . . . I thought you were a nonsmoker. Right.
> *(pause)*

John looks across.

> JOHN (CONT'D)
>
> Sorry. Can you follow me? Do you understand what I'm saying?

                         NADIA

Yes.

                         JOHN

Good. Or should I speak slower?

                         NADIA

Yes.

                         JOHN

Do you follow or should I speak slower?

                         NADIA

Yes.

He looks across. Back at the road. He changes gear.

                         JOHN

Uh . . . are you a giraffe?

                         NADIA

Yes.

John turns to face the road ahead.

                         JOHN

        (to himself)
        Oh, Jesus.

He drives in silence.

                    JOHN (CONT'D)

Oh, Jesus Christ.

Suddenly she winds the window down and vomits out of the speeding car. John panics and swerves onto the hard shoulder amidst loud horn blasts.

ext. motorway. day.

From a bridge we see a big truck looming down on the little car. It fires all its halogens and sounds its Klaxons. The MG swerves lanes, pulls across the hard sholder, and comes to a stop two wheels on the grassy shoulder.

ext. hard shoulder. day.

Seen from the other hard shoulder, through speeding traffic, John navigates his way 'round the MG in the chucking-down rain.

ext. hard shoulder/grass verge. day.

John finds her kneeling on the grassy shoulder, throwing up. He puts a hand on her shoulder, but she stands up quickly, maintaining an icy dignity considering what has just happened.

ext. john's close. day.

It has stopped raining and the pavements and lawns are steaming.

A group of young boys are playing cricket in the road. They clear as an orange MG pulls into the close, and into the drive of the little house at the end.

As John climbs out of his car he eyes the boys. The boys eye him and his new friend.

int. john's house. hallway. day.

The front door closes behind them. John and Nadia stand in the silence of his hallway.

There is a small banner hanging there: "Welcome Nadia." They study the banner together, gravely.

int. john's upstairs landing. day.

He puts her suitcase down on the landing, and opens a door. Without looking inside:

JOHN

Bathroom.

He closes it.

int. john's bedroom. day.

Standing in the doorway of John's bedroom.

JOHN

Bedroom.

There it is. The double bed. John frowns gravely.

Without warning, he marches out. She comes out onto the landing to catch John, plus suitcase, kicking open another door and vanishing inside.

int. nadia's bedroom. day.

Nadia peers around the door to find John standing next to a narrow monklike single bed.

JOHN

The uh . . . the other bedroom . . .

She looks at it, then up at John. She turns and walks out.

Now she's back, with her camouflaged carryall, dumps it onto the floor, heaves the suitcase onto the bed and, smoking no-hands, starts unpacking. John plugs in the lamp by the bed. To show Nadia how it works he switches it on, off, on, off, and then feels stupid.

JOHN (CONT'D)

I'll get an ashtray.

With John gone, Nadia stops unpacking. She walks to the window and stares out over the rooftops of the estate.

cut to:

int. living room. day.

John on the telephone with his back to us.

JOHN

This is John Buckingham from St. Albans. I need to speak to you absolutely urgently. There's been a mistake. She doesn't speak English. It's . . . call me back as soon as possible. It's critical.

He hangs up.

int. john's house. stairs/landing. day.

John climbs the stairs holding a saucer for an ashtray. He knocks

12

lightly on the spare room door.

int. nadia's bedroom/landing. day.

Nadia is lying asleep on the bed in only her black underwear. We duck straight back out.

int. nadia's bedroom. day.

He puts his head back 'round the door as if there's a real chance it will be shot off. She's facing away, arms folded, still holding the cigarette. It has burned out, leaving a long curl of ash on her bare hip.

He approaches the bed with immense trepidation, eases the cigarette from between her fingers, and drops it in the bin. He stares at her bare hip, with the ash on it. Holding the saucer under the ash, he blows on it gently. It takes three careful breaths before it drops in the saucer.

Unseen by John, her eyes are wide open as he steals out onto the landing. We stay with her a moment.

cut to:

int. john's house. kitchen. day.

John and Nadia sit opposite each other. She takes a mouthful. They catch each other's eye. And again. On the wall across, six ants careen in crazy circles. John spots an ant on his napkin, folds it, and scrunches it in his palm.

He puts his fork down.

JOHN

Your letters were in English. Good English. You said
you'd studied English.

*Nadia reaches down into her bag and pulls out a small box. She opens
it and takes out a ring.*

JOHN

I can't take that.

She holds it on her palm for him to take.

JOHN

I can't take that. I'm not really a ring guy.

*She takes his hand. He automatically yanks it away like he's been
burned. She takes his hand again and to stop it becoming unbearable,
he allows Nadia to push the ring onto his ring finger. It goes on easily.*

JOHN

Okay. No big deal. Thank you.
Yes, thanks. Thank you.

int. living room. night.

*John and Nadia sit next to each other on the couch watching TV.
John's gaze seems to go through the TV and a thousand yards beyond.
Nadia's knitting sits in her lap: the beginnings of a blood-red sweater.*

*Nadia points the remote control and flips through the channels: the
Money Programme; Antiques Roadshow; snooker, University
Challenge.*

*They watch University Challenge. John answers a question. Wrong
answer.*

14

ext. johns' house. night.

John's house lit up at night.

> JOHN (V/O)
> John Buckingham again. If anyone's there, can
> they please call me back as soon as possible. It's
> an emergency. Repeat, emergency.

int. john's bedroom. night.

*John lies in bed, fully clothed, in the moonlight. He is lost in his own
tense thoughts, until his eye catches something in his room.*

Someone is in the room with him.

*After a few frozen seconds, John climbs out of bed as casually as
possible and stands around.*

> JOHN
> You should go now. We'll talk in the morning.

*Nadia moves forward. John sidesteps her and hangs around by the
door, while she turns the lamp to the wall.*

*She comes to John, and he backs off, as if she has a force field. She
slowly backs him into the corner. His eyes widen but he can't speak.
He wants to but she's placed her hand across his mouth. She reaches
down and takes his hand, and draws it toward her, slowly tracing his
fingers across her breasts. She unbuttons her shirt and pulls his hand
inside.*

*He's breathing hard, her right hand still clasped over his mouth. Her
free hand lowers to press against him, and unzip his fly. He lets out a
moan.*

We concentrate on their faces. Above the silence all we can hear is John's breathing. Before long Nadia looks down. He's come.

Nadia turns and walks out, leaving John marooned, gasping in and blowing out, angry almost.

int. nadia's room. day.

The morning. Nadia opens her eyes in the sun-filled room. It takes a few moments to remember where she is.

ext. countryside. day.

John jogs along by a river in the countryside behind his house, wearing shorts and a T-shirt. His breath billows around him in the sharp morning air.

int. lounge. day.

John is on the phone.

> TELEPHONE
> You have reached From Russia with Love. If you are interested in any of our services. . . .

He hangs up.

int. john's bathroom. night.

Nadia looks at herself in the mirror and starts to cry. She sits on the edge of the bath, looking lonely and lost. She says something in Russian and pulls herself together.

int. john's house. landing. day.

John stands with his ear to the bathroom door. The shower's on.

int. nadia's bedroom. day.

It's empty. He slips inside.

Stuff everywhere. Cigarette cartons, several lighters, spare wool, suitcase, rucksack. Huge poster of Bruce Springsteen on the wall.

Warily, he opens the bedside drawer: different-colored bras and knickers.

In her open suitcase lies a small wooden chest. He lifts it out and puts it on the bed, hesitates, then opens it.

A pair of Russian army field binoculars. He puts them on the bed beside him. A small silver pistol, the size of a Derringer. He studies it, and pulls the trigger. It's a cigarette lighter.

A brochure of prospective husbands provided by the marriage agency. After a dozen or so photos he comes across his page but the photo has been cut out. He sees his name in the strange lettering, under the hole.

int. john's house. bathroom. day.

Nadia in the shower, eyes shut, water pouring over her face.

int. nadia's room. day.

John flicks through a stack of photographs. One of Nadia as a young girl in a meadow, with binoculars around her neck. John looks at the same binoculars on the bed next to him. He turns them over in his hands.

He looks through them. He slowly lowers them. He's seen something. He stands and crosses the room.

On the mantelpiece, in a silver frame, is his picture, cut from the brochure. He holds it in his hands.

The shower has stopped. In a panic he replaces the picture, the photographs, the gun lighter, the brochure, and the binoculars.

int. john's house. landing. day.

Nadia leaves the bathroom, hair wrapped in a towel, and heads straight toward us.

int. nadia's bedroom. day.

John shuts the chest, drops it back into the suitcase. The photo of the binoculars girl is on the pillow. He whips it under the bed just as Nadia enters.

She doesn't seem surprised to see him standing there, in her room, in his T-shirt and running shorts.

JOHN

Nadia. This isn't going to work.
I'm sorry. It's been a terrible mistake. You must go.

He takes the ring off and holds it out to her. She doesn't take it. He puts it on the bed.

JOHN

I'm booking a flight for tomorrow. I'm sorry.

jump cut to:

int. nadia's bedroom. day.

John and Nadia tumble onto her bed, Nadia tearing off his tee shirt. She gets on top.

ext. john's close. day.

The milkman hops a low fence between two houses. He waves to a man watering his rose bushes.

int. nadia's bedroom. day.

John and Nadia having sex. They don't take their eyes off each other.

ext. john's close. day.

A mother corrals her schoolchildren into a Volvo. They don't want to go.

int. nadia's bedroom. day.

John and Nadia having sex.

> BRANCH MANAGER (V/O)
> John Buckingham, deputy head of new business. Yearly report.

ext. st. albans. day.

Shoppers come and go. We see the outside of the TOWN AND COUNTRY ALLIED BANK.

> BRANCH MANAGER (V/O)
> John listens and comprehends well. When communicating he selects the most efficient methods and displays first-class communication skills in dealing with both customers and colleagues.

int. bank. day.

We move fast through the banking hall to the farthest counter. The blind snaps up to reveal John, wearing a smart suit.

> CLARE
> So John, did you have a good weekend?

> JOHN
> Uh. Yeah. Pretty good.

> CLARE
> Do anything special?

> JOHN
> Uh. No.

> BRANCH MANAGER (V/O)
> In January John narrowly missed promotion to head of New Business at the branch . . .

int. branch manager's office. day.

A prize ceremony—Clare is awarded a framed certificate and a photograph is taken. John is in the background, clapping.

BRANCH MANAGER V/O

. . . but was rewarded in March when he became a
trusted holder of the keys to the vault.

A prize ceremony—John is handed a set of keys and a photograph is taken.

int. bank vault. day.

John loads money into the safe.

BRANCH MANAGER (V/O)

This was to mark ten years' on-the-floor service.

int. branch manager's office. day.

John sits in front of a large desk.

BRANCH MANAGER (V/O)

Customer relations. Although John is sometimes
reticent to engage with customers, on one occasion
John showed first-class communication skills in a
delicate customer situation.

int. john's house. day.

Nadia walks into the kitchen in a dressing gown.

BRANCH MANAGER (V/O)

Problem solving. John identifies problems within
appropriate time frames. Most of the time he develops
several alternative solutions to problems. He usually
resolves or minimizes most problems before they grow
into larger problems . . .

int. john's house. kitchen. day.

Nadia opens a kitchen cupboard and stares inside at John's groceries.

> BRANCH MANAGER (V.O.)
> If a problem will not go away, John must not hesitate
> to notify his superiors. Initiative. John is reasonably
> quick to volunteer whenever others need help.
> Although he is sometimes reluctant and or unwilling
> to ask for it himself . . .

She opens some pickled onions and pops one in her mouth.

int. john's house. living room. day.

Cradling the jar of pickles, she scans his bookshelf.

> BRANCH MANAGER (V/O)
> As a local boy, John is a recognizable face to customers
> and so a valuable tool in maintaining lasting relation-
> ships with customers.

*She sees Bluffer's Guide to the Internet. She opens an old copy
of* The Lion, the Witch and the Wardrobe. *Inside is written
"John Buckingham Class 3F."*

int. john's house. john's bedroom. day.

She opens the wardrobe. In a shoebox she finds some photos.

> BRANCH MANAGER (V/O)
> . . . Although John still has some reluctance to/or has
> problems in carving out new relationships face-to-face.

*One of John as a little boy, holding a football, flanked by his parents.
On the back someone has written "Summer 1973."*

*There is a photo of John, about three years ago, arm in arm with a
plain, thin-looking girl, with small eyes. Another of him kissing her
on the cheek.*

int. nat west bank. branch manager's office. day.

John listening. Close-up on the branch manager's mouth.

> BRANCH MANAGER (V/O)
> Judgment. John makes able decisions
> in most areas of his job.

int. john's house. john's bedroom. day.

*Nadia sees something at the bottom of the cupboard. She bends
down to retrieve a black dustbin liner. She reaches in and pulls out
a small stack of hardcore pornographic magazines.*

> BRANCH MANAGER (V/O)
> John follows instructions conscientiously and
> responds well to personal directions, and in most situa-
> tions assumes responsibility for his own actions and
> outcomes.

*She upends the bag and a half dozen videos fall out. She picks up a
magazine and begins flicking through it impassively.*

int. john's house. living room. day.

Nadia downstairs kneels in front of the TV and slips a video into the machine. Nadia's face is lit up by the screen. The sound of sex.

BRANCH MANAGER (CONT'D)
On the whole, John grasps the central priciples of bank-ing for the new century. He understands and responds to the power structure on the floor. In conclusion, John should be satisfied with his performance. This has been a sound, workmanlike year for him, much the same as last year.

Nadia pops a pickled onion in her mouth and watches. We see the images close and pixellated, as we did the marriage videos in the titles. It's a bondage scene; the woman wears a gag.

int. branch manager's office. day.

John back in the room. The report has finished and the manager is scrutinizing him in silence.

JOHN
Thank you. I think that's very fair.

int/ext. john's car (moving). day.

John drives his MG through the center of town, the low orange sun on his face. He puts on some metal-framed sunglasses.

ext. john's close. day.

The MG pulls into the driveway. John opens the glove compartment and removes the ring Nadia gave him, and puts it back on. He collects a brown paper package from the passenger seat.

24

int. john's kitchen. day.

*John and Nadia at the supper table. She is knitting the jumper.
Despite the silence, John seems more relaxed, in shirtsleeves and
loosened tie.*

*He puts his fork down, and places the brown bag on the table,
pushing it across to Nadia. She opens it and removes a big hardback
Russian-English dictionary. John smiles and nods "Open it." She flicks
through it.*

*She turns it over in her hands, nods, puts the book down, reaches
under the table, and surfaces with the stack of porn magazines.
She puts them on the table next to the dictionary.*

John beholds the pile. Anal Roundup is on top.

He rises slowly from the table and sleepwalks from the kitchen.

cut to:

int. john's hall/stairs/landing/bathroom. day.

*John, frozen-headed, floats down the hall, up the stairs, into the
bathroom, locks the door, sits on the toilet.*

int. john's kitchen. day.

*Downstairs Nadia clears the dishes. The porn stack still sits on the
table, beside the dictionary.*

ext. john's house. dusk.

The bathroom light is on.

int. landing. night.

It's dark. The bathroom door opens a crack. The coast clear, he dashes for the cover of his bedroom.

int. john's bedroom. night.

John opens the door to his bedroom. Nadia is sitting on the bed.

She is playing with his tie 'round her neck. Slowly she loosens it. Holding it in her hands she examines the strange little bank logo on it, before deliberately wrapping it 'round her wrists and pulling it taut.

She gives him a long, level look. John stares back at her for several seconds. Slowly, he closes the door on us.

TRAINER (V/O)

And, go.

cut to:

int. room in the bank. day.

A close up of John's face. He closes his eyes, falls backward, and is caught in the arms of a colleague.

TRAINER

Very good. How does that feel, John?

JOHN

It feels good. Weird.

                              TRAINER
         It's called "trust and letting go."

John nods.

                         TRAINER (CONT'D)
         Trust and letting go.

*A simple guitar theme begins, and plays over the following montage
sequence:*

int. john's bedroom. night.

*A pair of knitting needles are pulled out of a ball of red wool and
dragged down John's bare chest.*

ext. john's close. day.

A milkman does his rounds.

ext. john's close. day.

*A mother corrals her schoolchildren into a Volvo. They don't want
to go.*

int. John's house. john's bedroom. night.

*Close up on a man's hands tying a tie tight around a woman's
wrist. Pull back to a close-up of Nadia's face, her eyes fixed on
John.*

ext. open countryside. day.

John running by the river.

int. John's house. john's bedroom. night.

John and Nadia have sex.

int. bank. day.

John sits at his desk, staring blankly into the distance.

int. john's bedroom. day.

A half-completed red sweater is laid out on the bed.

int. john's house. john's bedroom. dusk.

John, at dusk, tied to the bed with his two bank ties. Nadia is on top. They are having sex.

ext. country lane. day.

A helecopter shot of John running.

int. john's close. day.

Kids playing cricket in John's close. A boy hits the ball and others chase it as it bounces off cars.

int. john's house. john's bedroom. night.

John watches Nadia rise from his bed after sex and walk to the
window where she looks out at the rain.

ext. john's close. day.

It is pouring with rain. John and Nadia emerge from the house. She
is barefoot, only wearing her coat. He has shirt and trousers on. They
run to the ice-cream van and order two ice creams.

ext. john's garden. day.

Rain coming down in John's garden. The pair sit under the shelter of
the back porch. John has his hands out as Nadia is winding red wool
into a ball. The jumper is half-finished.

int. john's living room. day.

Extreme close-up: an ant crawls up a knitting needle.

int. kitchen. day.

John pops his head 'round the kitchen door, where Nadia is
killing ants on the table, with her dictionary. He smiles. She smiles
back.

int. living room. day.

A beautiful morning. Through the patio window, John watches
Nadia in the garden, sitting on the lawn reading her dictionary
in the sunlight. In dungarees with her hair up, she looks very
young.

ext. garden. day.

*He walks warily out into the sunlight. She looks up, then back to the
big book in her lap. He places the tea next to her on the grass.*

> JOHN

Are you okay?

*She looks at him, then down at her tome. She speaks slowly, in a heavy
accent:*

> NADIA

Today is bath day.

> JOHN

Sorry?

She studies her book. Looks up.

> NADIA

Today is bath day.

He shakes his head.

> JOHN

Bath day?

She nods.

> JOHN

I don't understand.

> NADIA

Happy bath day.

The penny drops.

JOHN

Today?

She frowns. John leafs through the dictionary.

JOHN

Syevodnya?

NADIA

Syevodnya.

JOHN

Happy birthday. Happy birthday.

He puts his hand on her shoulder.

NADIA

Party.
(pause)
Party. *Syevodnya.*

John nods, smiling.

JOHN

Yes. Party. Party, *Syevodnya.*

She lights a cigarette from the butt of her last. Blows smoke.

int. john's living room. night.

*Nadia sits alone at the dining room table. Suddenly the lights
go out. John enters, carrying a small birthday cake glowing with
candles. The light throws huge shadows on the walls and flickers
across their faces. He sets the cake down on the table and sits down
opposite Nadia.*

31

JOHN (SINGS)

Happy birthday to you
Happy birthday to you
Happy birthday, dear Nadia—

The front doorbell rings. A loud long burst. Nadia's face transforms into a big grin. She hurries out into the hall, leaving John alone with the cake.

Nadia whooping and shouting excitedly.

Other voices. Shouting. Shouting in Russian.

(This happens offscreen)

NADIA

Boze moi! Yuri!
(Oh my God! Yuri!)

YURI

Tsipljonok!
(Chicken!)

NADIA

Priehal! Neverojatno! Ty deystvitelno priehal!
(You came! I don't believe it! You came!)

YURI

A ty dumala ja zabudu o tvojom dne rozdenija?
(You think I'd forget your birthday?)

A man bursts in carrying Nadia in his arms.

YURI (CONT'D)

Ty u menja krasavitsa.
(to Alexei)

Ja tebe govoril, chto ona krasavitsa.
(You're beautiful.)
(to Alexei)
(I told you she was beautiful.)

He spins her 'round in the candlelight, kisses her, puts her down, and goes to the table where he blows out the candles. They are plunged into darkness.

(Also in darkness, i.e., offscreen)

                              NADIA

        Neverojatno!
        (I can't believe it.)

                              YURI

    Pravda klassno? Prjamo kak v skazke!
    (It's cool, isn't it? It's like a dream!)

Lots of whooping and laughing. A Zippo flares up and illuminates some faces, all laughing.

                              YURI

    Takoi krasivoi ja tebja escho ne videl.
    (You are prettier than ever.)

                                                    cut to:

John's hand groping along the wall. It finds the light switch.

There are two men here. One small and wiry, one big and dark, like Rasputin, in a long leather coat. They each carry rucksacks and a guitar case.

33

YURI

You must be John. You seem very nice. Excuse me.

In Russian, the first man introduces Nadia to the other man, who is relighting the candles with a Zippo. It seems they haven't met before.

YURI (CONT'D)

*Nadia. Horosho. Pozaluista, poznakomsja s moim
novym zakadychnym drugom, Alekseem. Aleksei—
eto Nadia.*
(Nadia. Okay. I'd like you to meet my new buddy,
Alexei. Alexei—this is Nadia.)

ALEXEI

Ochen prijatno s vami poznakomitsa.
(Pleased to meet you.)

NADIA

Mne toze ochen prijatno.
(Pleased to meet you, too.)

YURI

On iz . . . chort poberi. Otkuda ty rodom?
(He's from . . . shit. Where are you from?)

ALEXEI

Iz Novgoroda.
(Novgorod.)

YURI

Iz Novgoroda. Pridurok.
(Novgorod. He's crazy.)

ALEXEI

S dniom rozdenija.
(Happy birthday.)

34

NADIA

Spasibo. Ja daze pokrasnela.
(Thank you. I'm blushing.)

The tall man, Alexei, pulls out a bottle of vodka and hands it to Yuri who passes it to John.

YURI

How's that? We can't drink our piss, can we?

JOHN

Hang on, hang on, sorry but, like, who are you?

YURI

You must find some glasses, small, for toast.

JOHN

What are you doing here?

Yuri stops.

YURI

Sorry. You've lost me . . .

Yuri speaks to Nadia in fast Russian.

YURI

Podozhdzi, podozhdzi. Ohn ni govorit po Rousski?
(Hold on. He doesn't speak Russian?)

NADIA

Njet.
(No.)

YURI

(to John)

35

You don't speak Russian? *Pratsteetye!*
This explains your cold eyes.

Nadia begins gabbing to Yuri in Russian.

NADIA

Nu skazi . . . skazi, chto eto moi druzja. Kak skazat'
druzja poangliyski?
(Say uh . . . say these are my friends. How do you say
"friends" in English?)

YURI

"Friends."

NADIA

(to John)
"Frenzy."

JOHN

Yes, I know.

YURI

(points to himself)
Yuri.
(Rasputin)
Alexei. Alexei and Yuri.

Alexei speaks.

ALEXEI

Pomoyou, boudzyet ochen prosto.
(I think this will be pretty easy.)

JOHN

What did he say?

YURI

He say he feel safe here.

NADIA

Horosho, horosho, Yuri. Aa.. Skazi emu, chto ja hotela skazat', shto tui.
(Okay, okay, Yuri. Uh . . . tell him I wanted to tell him you . . .)

Nadia talks fast to Yuri.

YURI

She say she want to tell you but her English is shit. No one speaks Russian, so very hard for her. Light, please.

Alexei turns off the light again. They sing "Happy Birthday" in Russian. Nadia blows out her candles. They are plunged back into darkness.

YURI (CONT'D)

Hvatsit, Ribyatah! Davai k dzelou.
(Okay, guys. Let's get on with it.)

John turns the light on again. Yuri is already sitting down.

JOHN

I need to know who you are first, please.

YURI

Oh.
(he stands)
We are Russian.

JOHN

Yes. I know.

YURI

Good.
(he sits down)

JOHN

And?

YURI

And what? You mean from the beginning? Jesus. Can I, uh, okay, as we say in Russia, can I cut long story short? Okay. Nadia is my little cousin. Except she's not. But we say cousin. This is for you.

He hands John another bottle of vodka.

JOHN

Hold on—

YURI

Toast first, then we talk seriously, I can see you are serious about us.

Vodka is splashed into four glasses. Yuri raises his glass and shouts a toast in Russian: "Vashe Zdarov'ye!" They down their vodka, John sips at his, then realizes he must finish it.

Yuri makes as if to throw his in the fireplace.

YURI

Just kidding.

Sausages, cheese, bread, and pickle bottles rain onto the table from Yuri's rucksack.

YURI (CONT'D)
Sloushai—mui zdyes privyezli koeshto shtob' tui ni

skouchala po domou.
(We've bought you some goodies so that you wouldn't
feel homesick.)

JOHN

(to Yuri)
So hang on. You're both Nadia's cousins?

YURI

(shaking his head)
Of course not. Alexei, he's my problem.

JOHN

Right.

YURI

We better watch him. He's crazy.

JOHN

Right.

YURI

I am actor, he is actor, although he is actor-stroke-
musician. I just noodle along, I'm not so good. He
makes me look like a retard. He smokes me. I don't
mean he smokes me.

Yuri mimes giving a blow job.

YURI (CONT'D)

I mean he smokes me. You say "smoke" in England?

He mimes the blow-job again.

JOHN

No.

39

YURI

Right. So I can say he smokes me. So.

Pause.

JOHN

So?

YURI

So. So I come to England with other actors to make
shows, I meet this freak from Novgorod, I tell him
of you and Chicken and birthday cake and here we
are.

YURI (TO NADIA)

Emu takaja versija podhodit? On smotrit na menja tak,
kak budto ja tolko chto nagadil (nasral) emu na kovjor.
(Is he cool with this? He's looking at me like I just shat
on his rug.)

NADIA

On vsegda tak smotrit.
(He always looks like that.)

Yuri speaks to Nadia in Russian, she replies looking at John.

JOHN

What was that?

YURI

I asked her if you were happy to see us. I find it hard to
tell with you.

JOHN

Yes, it's okay. Thank you for the food.

Nadia lights a cigarette. John notices that on both wrists she has bold, red marks from the ties.

NADIA

Ja dumaju, chto on nemnogo zastenchiv. Ty dolzhen po-horoshemu zastavit' ego vypolzty iz svoei skorlupy.
(I think he's a bit shy. You've got to coax him out of his shell.)

YURI

Ne somnevajus.
(I bet.)

Yuri winks at Alexei who stonewalls. John is thrown, panicking that one of them will notice the marks.

JOHN

So how long will you be in England?

YURI

Plans are for architects, politicians, and so forth.

JOHN

You must have a visa or something . . .

YURI

You're asking for my documents?

JOHN

No, no . . .

Yuri laughs, translates for Alexei.

YURI

Ty ponjal! On prosit pokazat' moi chortov (jobany) pasport.
(Get this. He's asking for my fucking papers.)

And they both get a big laugh out of this. Yuri gets his passport out and makes a big show of presenting it to John.

>   YURI (CONT'D)
> *Na, smotri, ja ves' kak na ladoni. Tolko popravilsa na paru kilo.*
> (They're all there. I've put on a few pounds.)

>   NADIA
> *Ne drazni ego.*
> (Don't tease him.)

But John keeps glancing at the marks on Nadia's wrists.

>   YURI
> We are all Europeans here. Europe, Tony Blair, and Maggie Thatcher!

Yuri raises his glass and they all drink to Tony Blair and Margaret Thatcher. John drinks his vodka in two hot gulps.

>   YURI
> So. You have nothing to say to your fiancée ? Maybe to wife of forty years it's understandable. Come on. You speak, I will translate.

John looks glazed. The room falls silent.

>   JOHN
> Hello.

Yuri translates.

>   YURI
> *Privyet.*

She replies.

42

NADIA

Privyet.

YURI

She says 'Hello' to you. Go for it John!

JOHN

Uh. Do you like England?

YURI

Classic!
(he translates)
Anglia tsibyeh nravitsa?

NADIA

Da.

YURI

Thank God. She says, "Yes!"

John nods. He watches Nadia tap her ash. The wrist again.

JOHN

Uh . . .

They all wait. Yuri nods encouragingly.

JOHN (CONT'D)

I can't think of anything.

Nadia speaks in Russian to Yuri.

NADIA

Skazi emu, chto ja hochu otkryt' odin sekret.
(Tell him I have a secret to tell.)

                    YURI
She says she has secret to tell.

                    JOHN
    What?

Nadia speaks.

                   NADIA
    Skazi emu, chto ja sledila za nim v aeroportu.
    (Tell him I watched him at the airport.)

John waits uncomfortably. Silence.

                    YURI
    She says she watched you at airport.

John stops.

                    JOHN
    When?

                   NADIA
    Ja videla, kak ty stojal rjadom s ograzdenijem.
    (I saw you standing there, by the gate.)

                    YURI

                (TRANSLATING)
    "I saw you waiting there, by the gate."

                    JOHN
    I . . .

                    YURI
    "I have these uh . . ." She explains to you . . ."

                    44

When I was a little girl my father had these beautiful
old . . . glasses."

Like . . . I don't know the word. Like for watching uh . . .
for watching the birds.

We see John's face.

> JOHN
>
> Binoculars.

> YURI
>
> "Binoculars. He had these binocularshe has kept from
> the war.

cut to:

ext. summer meadow. day.

reprise, scene 1.

*A young girl runs through a summer meadow with a pair of Russian
army field binoculars around her neck.*

> YURI (CONT'D)
>
> "The day before I left Russia my father gave me the old
> binoculars."

*With the binoculars pressed to her face, she spies butterflies, birds,
a rabbit. She stops running and aims the binoculars up, up, into
the sun.*

> WOMAN'S VOICE
>
> *(Distant)*
> Nadia . . . Na-dia!!

int. john's living room. night (cont'd).

Yuri translates.

> YURI
>
> "He said that when I saw you I was to stand far away
> and look at you through the binoculars, and if you were
> a bad person I could run away."

Nadia looks at the table.

> YURI (CONT'D)
> She says she took a picture. In the head.

*John watches Nadia looking at the table. She glances up once and
catches his eye.*

ext. john's garden. night.

*The small party has moved outside to the patio, where they sit
around a low wooden table in the mellow candlelight. A huge late
Summer moon hangs over the fields. Alexei tinkles beautifully on
his guitar.*

He stops asks a question in Russian.

> ALEXEI
>
> *Ja znaju. Sprosi ego, zachem emu ponadobilos iskat'
> zheny v rossii.*
> (I know. Ask him why he has to send off to Russia for
> a wife.)

> JOHN
>
> What was that?

YURI

Oh. Nothing.

JOHN

Tell me.

YURI

No. It is too judgmental.

JOHN

Tell me what he said.

YURI

He says why did you send to
Russia for a wife.

Silence. John suddenly looks sick.

YURI

You are not ashamed of it? It's no
surprise to want to love.

JOHN

No. It's not that.

YURI

Do you believe in love?

JOHN

I suppose it's . . . I mean, define your terms.

YURI

It's very strange. How many people are truly themselves
with their love? It is greatest human disaster and it is
never in the newspapers. There are no Marches Against
Heartache, no Ministries Against Loneliness, no

Concerts Against Disappointment. We look away. And still we know in secret that nothing is more important to us. The one thing we all share but don't say.

Look, John, I will show you something.

He takes a plate and starts reaching for the food.

> YURI (CONT'D)
> Here, look, something beautiful from Russia. Here is Life: there, take it.

John accepts the plate.

> YURI (CONT'D)
> Here is bread. *Khylep.* This is work.
> We all need this: here, eat.

John eats.

> YURI (CONT'D)
> Good. But we cannot survive with just work, so here is meat and blood. *Myasa.* This is family and country, flesh, strength: eat.

John bites the sausage.

> YURI (CONT'D)
> But again, this is not life. Here is joy and pain. *Chyesnok.* Without these life has no flavor, is too serious. Eat.

John nibbles some pickled garlic.

> YURI (CONT'D)
> But this *votka.*
> *(Pause)*

Is love. Only this magic changes you inside. The moon
and the stars and the sun.

*Yuri offers John the glass. He looks at Nadia, takes it, and swigs it
down in one gulp. He looks across at Nadia, wiping his mouth, his
eyes watering. She looks back at him.*

Alexei begins softly singing a song. As he sings:

YURI (CONT'D)
This is a love song, a soldier's song to his beloved.
Alexei, he's *Afghanstya,* a veteran of Afghanistan. He
saw terrible things . . .

*They listen to the beautiful, sad voice. For the second verse Yuri joins
in, a slow, stirring lament. For the end, Nadia joins in too and the
three of them begin harmonizing beautifully. John watches in the
candlelight.*

cut to:

ext. john's garden. night.

*John, Nadia, and Alexei pose with the cake. Nadia puts her
arm 'round John and Alexei. With a FLASH! Yuri takes a
Polaroid.*

*The guitar theme returns as we see the Polaroid on the table in
close-up, developing speeded up. John comes into focus, beaming.*

int. living room. night.

*We track across the sleeping faces of Yuri and Alexei tucked into their
sleeping bags with guitar cases for pillows.*

int. john's bedroom. night.

John and Nadia make love, kissing tenderly.

ext. open countryside. dawn.

John jogs along a track in the woods.

*Suddenly Alexei appears into the shot from the right, also running.
He is wearing his coat, no shirt, trousers and his big boots. John
glances across, and Alexei looks back. They run side by side, without
speaking.*

*Soon John stops. Alexei stops, too, and the two of them stand around
panting.*

*Alexei slaps John on the back, a little too hard. He tries to box John.
Then he drop-kicks a tree, encouraging John to have a go too. After
some time John vaguely indicates that he's heading back and does.
Alexei is left alone. He pats his coat down for cigarettes and finds one.*

ext. high street. day.

Shoppers mill about.

int. bank. men's toilet. day.

*The branch manager finishes relieving himself at a urinal. We
pan across to John, sitting in a cubicle. He has the Russian-English
dictionary open on his lap and is writing a note in faltering Russian.*

int. bank. day.

John is at his desk. His phone rings. He answers it. Nadia whispers something in Russian. John listens intently and looks around. "Nadia . . . ?" John sits there, surrounded by his colleagues, listening to Nadia breathe.

int. branch manager's office. day.

The branch manager sits at his desk. Clare pops her head 'round the door.

CLARE

John's had to pop out to see a client.

int. john's car [moving]. day.

John drives home.

int. kitchen/conservatory. day.

John walks through the kitchen into the conservatory. Hanging from the ceiling is a rabbit skin. John stares at it, then notices Nadia's red wool leading from the rabbit skin, out of the door, and stretching across the garden to the stile and the field beyond.

ext. forest. day.

John follows the wool, tied to trees and fence-posts, through a big silent wood, the low sun flaring and catching his white work shirt.

ext. forest. day.

POV through binoculars, of John, a long way off and squinting into the sun.

ext. forest. day.

Nadia lowers the binoculars and looks past us.

ext. forest clearing. day.

John spots some figures lying on the grass in the distance. He heads toward them, and watches them for a moment from thirty yards away.

ext. forest clearing. day.

Alexei, Yuri, and Nadia sit in a small clearing. A blanket, cushions, bread, and vodka are scattered around. Yuri is strumming a guitar. Alexei and Nadia are laughing and chatting. He removes a small twig from her hair and flattens it under his big hand. John watches the gesture, it's so intimate they could be lovers.

> YURI
>
> *(calls)*
> John. We can see you. Come here. Come here,
> John.

ext. forest clearing. day.

John steps out of his hiding place and approaches the group. Alexei has Nadia falling about laughing about something. He smiles at her, then nods to John.

ALEXEI

Bystro. Davai escho kusok krolika.
(Quick. Here comes another rabbit.)

Pieces of cooked rabbit lie in tin foil.

ALEXEI

Nu chto, hochesh' escho krolchatiny?
(You want some more rabbit meat, eh?)

JOHN

I thought you were leaving today.

YURI

To be indoors on such a day. It's crime.

Nadia stretches back to sunbathe. Alexei takes the knife he has just finished cleaning and holds the cold, wide blade flat above Nadia's bare stomach. Just before pressing it down he looks across at John. Nadia yelps and sits up.

NADIA

Ubljudok!
(Bastard!)

ALEXEI

Chego?
(What?)

YURI

Chto on sdelal?
(What did he do?)

NADIA

On kholodny kak ljod. Perestan'.
(That was freezing. Stop it.)

53

They laugh, and Yuri joins in. John laughs uneasily.

Alexei notices marks on Nadia's midriff. He asks her about them in Russian.

ALEXEI

Otkuda u tebja eti sledy?
(Where did you get those marks?)

NADIA

Chegro? Da tak. Niotuda. Trava, navernoe. Dolzhno byt' syp'.
(What? Oh. Nowhere. It's the grass. It must be a rash.)

John goes white, unable to understand Nadia's explanation. He has no idea what she told him.

ext. lake in forest. day.

At sunset, the four run toward a lake in their underwear. They jump and dive in, and begin splashing each other.

NADIA

Voda ledjanaja.
(It's freezing.)

YURI

Khorosho dlja zakalki.
(It's good for you.)

John duck dives under the water and swims through the sunlit-streaked green water. We see him under the water, swimming toward us, caught by the sun's rays.

John surfaces, and wipes the water from his eyes. He spots Alexei and Nadia playing in the water.

>   ALEXEI
> *Idzi syouda. Ou tsibyah shto-to na litseh.*
> (Come here. You've got something on your face.)

>   NADIA
> *Gde?*
> (Where?)

Alexei grabs her and throws her in the air and she comes down with a splash.

>   NADIA (CONT'D)
> *Piristan'. Mne bolno.*
> (Cut it out. That hurt.)

John treads water nearby. He watches them both hold their noses . . .

>   NADIA (CONT'D)
> *Raz . . . dva . . . tri.*
> (One . . . two . . . three.)

. . . and disappear under the surface.

They've both vanished. John ducks under the water. John's underwater POV: It's too murky to see anything. The two surface, breathing hard, laughing. John watches them.

>   ALEXEI
> *Ya vuigral.*
> (I won.)

NADIA

Ya vuigral.
(I won.)

ALEXEI

Akh tak?
(Oh yeah?)

Alexei holds Nadia tight and looks like he might even kiss her. But instead he ducks her and holds her under the water.

John treads water nearby. She's been under a long time.

JOHN

Hey!

John begins to swim toward Alexei. Just as he gets near, Alexei lets Nadia surface, coughing and spluttering. She shouts at Alexei in Russian, angry.

NADIA

Kakogo khrena? Mne nechem bylo dyshat'.
(What the fuck are you doing? I couldn't breathe.)

ALEXEI

Chego?
(What?)

NADIA

Ni kapli ne smeshno . . . Mne nechem bylo dyshat, ty, ubljudok . . .
(It's not funny . . . I couldn't breathe, you fucker . . .)

Alexei makes for her again, but she pushes him away, twice, almost slapping him.

NADIA

Prekrati menja lapat'.
(Stop touching me.)

She is very uncomfortable. She swims away.

Yuri admonishes his friend in Russian.

YURI

Ei ty. Ja tebe skazal ne pridurivatsa. Ty chto eto delaesh?
A? Ty chto delaesh?
(Hey. I told you not to fuck around. What did you do?
Eh? What did you do?)

Alexei stares at John, then swims off powerfully back toward the
shore.

YURI

He's just having fun. He's maybe too strong, you
know . . .

John watches Nadia walk out of the lake toward her clothes.

int. john's bedroom. night.

John walks into his bedroom. Nadia is on the bed with a dictionary.
She puts it down. She speaks very slowly.

NADIA

They go. John. They go.

JOHN

What's wrong?

57

NADIA

They go.

JOHN

Of course. They go. Yes. Yes.

NADIA

They go.

int. john's living room. night.

John stands at the end of the two sleeping bags.

JOHN

I'm sorry. I'm really sorry, but I'm going to have to ask you to leave.

YURI

Oh, I'm sorry John.

JOHN

It's not you.

YURI

It's my fault. Maybe I should have come alone.

JOHN

It's okay. You can stay tonight.

YURI

I'm sorry. I don't know him that much. Okay, I see you tomorrow morning, then we go.

JOHN

Good night, Yuri.

YURI
Thank you, John. Thank you very much. Thank you.

Alexei stares at John as he backs out of the room.

int. john's bedroom. night.

John closes his bedroom door and slips back into bed. Nadia is asleep.

cross-fade to:

Nadia is facing him now, asleep. He gently strokes her hair from her face.

int. john's bedroom. day.

John opens his eyes. He rolls over toward Nadia, but she's already up and about.

Alone in his bedroom, John holds the now-finished jumper up to himself. He tries it on. It's a good four sizes too big, the arms are too long, and it hangs down to midthigh. He looks at himself in the mirror and smiles.

cut to:

int. john's house. stairs/hall/kitchen. day.

He pads downstairs in his pants, picks up his mail from the doormat. About to peruse his mail, he hears a crash in the kitchen.

59

Twenty feet away, down the hall, is Yuri, sitting on the kitchen floor, his back to the cooker. He's crying.

YURI

I'm sorry, John. I'm sorry.

JOHN

What's happened?

John hears Nadia cry out from inside the kitchen. He drops his mail and rushes forward.

int. kitchen. day.

Nadia is tied to a chair. Alexei pulls a gag tight around her mouth, and holds the knife to her throat.

JOHN

What are you doing?

Alexei charges at John and upturns the kitchen table, scattering things everywhere. Alexei shouts at Yuri in Russian.

ALEXEI

Khorosho. Seichas my zaimjomsa delom. Seichas my i zaimjomsa delom.
(Okay. Now we do it. Now we do it.)

Alexei shouts again.

ALEXEI

Seichas my i zaimjomsa nashim trekjatym delom.
(You're throwing me out?)

Nadia is frozen with terror.

JOHN

What's he doing? What the fuck are you doing? Leave
her alone.

Alexei addresses John.

ALEXEI

Skazhi emu, chtoby sel.
(Sit down! Tell him to sit down!)

YURI

He says sit down.

JOHN

What's he saying?

ALEXEI

(OVERLAPPING)
*Khorosho. Teper' my posmotrim. Teper' my posmotrim,
mat' vashu.*
(You think you can buy our women?)

YURI (CONT'D)
My vsjo-taki v gostjakh.
(We're guests here.)

Nadia begins crying.

The kettle boils.

JOHN

Tell him to stop and let her go, and we'll talk.

YURI

Ty chto eto sebje pozvoljaesh?
(Let me do this?)

ALEXEI

Teper' my mat' vashu posmotrim. Teper' my post-
motrium. Teper' my posmotrim, kakov on na samom
dele.
(Now we'll bloody see. See if he's got any balls.)

YURI

Ei tui, ostanovis, idiot priduroshny.
(Don't hurt her.)

Alexei knocks Yuri onto the floor and charges at John pushing
him into the chair and punching the wall hard beside John's
head.

ALEXEI

Skazi emu chtoby kupil sebe bljad.
(Tell him he has to pay for a whore.)

Alexei grabs Nadia's head.

ALEXEI

Vot etu bljad.
(Here's a whore for him.)

Alexei takes the kettle and holds it over Nadia's head. John
springs up.

JOHN

Put the fucking kettle down.

YURI

John—

JOHN

Put the fucking kettle down. Tell, Yuri, tell him put it
down . . .

He tilts the kettle, and a small amount of boiling water trickles onto Nadia's hair. She screams through the gag. John tries to reach across to her, but Alexei draws the knife and holds it to his face.

> JOHN
>
> What? What do you want?

Alexei speaks.

> ALEXEI
>
> *Badok. Deneg.*
> (Money.)

ext. high street. day.

Two Morris Dancers' sticks crack together against a blue sky.

The Morris Dancers perform in the middle of the busy precinct.

John strides past them down St. Albans High Street, carrying the two guitar cases, wearing his suit for work. His eyes look glazed, the busy street sounds around him muffled.

int. bank. day.

The doors slide apart and John enters his branch. The place is full of customers. He checks himself through the security door and into the back.

int. open-plan office. day.

John walks through the open-plan office. His branch manager is there with another bank official, and Clare.

BRANCH MANAGER

Ah, John. This is Robert Moseley, head of South
East New Business. Robert, this is John
Buckingham.

MOSELEY

Hello, John.

JOHN

Hello.

BRANCH MANAGER

I thought you could give us the tour this morning.
Sort of be our Indian guide.

JOHN

Right.

MOSELEY

(i.e., the guitars)
Do you play?

JOHN

Yes. I do.

CLARE

That's John. He's always surprising you with his hidden
talents.

MOSELEY

I used to be in a band. Keyboards. Sort of like very loud,
uh . . . very loud Marillion.

They laugh. Pause.

CLARE

(to John)
Well, maestro, give us a tune.

They laugh. Pause.

JOHN

I'll give you a tune later.

The branch manager takes John to one side and stage whispers:

BRANCH MANAGER

Take the ball and run with it, John.

int. bank corridor. day.

John leads the team down the corridor past the training room where his colleagues are busy with "trust and letting go."

JOHN

This is uh . . . This is the, uh . . .

A colleague passes carrying a file.

PASSING COLLEAGUE

Morning, John. Give us a tune.

JOHN

I'll give you a tune later.

int. training room. day.

They enter the training room.

JOHN

This is where we're doing "trust and, uh . . . trust and letting go."

MOSELEY

We're not doing this till the fourth quarter. Has it, uh . . . any results, has it been beneficial?

JOHN

Yes.

CLARE

It's weird at first. Sort of exciting and frightening at the same time. Wouldn't you say, John?

JOHN

Yes.

BRANCH MANAGER

We're starting to see results. This is Karen, who's uh . . . taking uh . . . it.

They say hello to each other and MOSELEY asks her a couple of questions.

JOHN

Excuse me.

int. corridor. day.

John nips out and fetches his guitar cases. He checks himself into the safe area. A Colleague passes him.

COLLEAGUE

Morning John. Hey. Moseley's here.

66

JOHN

I'll give you a tune later.

int. safe room door. day.

*John inserts his set of keys, opens the safe door, and goes inside,
closing it behind him. We see his stricken face peering through the
bars. Inside, he turns all the wheels of the combination locks on
the safe door and opens it successfully.*

int. training room. day.

Robert Moseley falls backward into the arms of an employee.

MOSELEY

It's weird, isn't it?

TRAINER

So if you'd like to swap places with your partners, we'll
do a bit of mutuality.

*A little bored, perhaps, Moseley gazes out through the glass window
of the training room into the corridor. He sees . . .*

int. corridor. day.

*John bowling out of the safe room backward, heaving two guitar
cases.*

int. training room. day.

Moseley, the branch manager, and Clare all watch . . .

int. corridor. day.

. . . John smile and swoop past them . . .

int. training room. day.

. . . as the three "trust and letting go" fallers crash to the ground in unison.

ext. side street. day.

The fire door of the bank is kicked open and John hauls ass toward us straight down the middle of the road, a guitar case in either hand, footsteps clapping loudly. Alarms sound, dogs bark.

ext. street corner. day.

He skis around a corner, and sprints up this other street.

ext. car park roof. day.

Running flat out across the car park. Yuri throws open the car door and John hurls one guitar case into the boot and another onto Yuri's lap. He dives in, turns the key in the ignition. The MG coughs and wheezes. He tries again. It spits and misfires.

JOHN
Come on, you big orange bastard! Live!

The third time it catches and lives. John grinds the gears and lurches off.

int. multistorey car park. day.

The Capri hurtles down the ramps.

ext. street. day.

It careens out of the car park, crashing into a motorcycle and a car, setting off alarms, and spilling oil all over the road. The car reverses from the collision and pulls off, hurtling down the side street.

int/ext. moving capri. day.

JOHN
Tell him, he's got what he wanted and to let her go.

YURI
Thank you, John. Thank you very much.

John looks in the rearview mirror and sees Alexei gently pull the tape from Nadia's mouth. She looks at John in the mirror, then turns to Alexei who kisses her on the mouth. She returns the kiss hungrily.

We close in on John, watching them in the mirror. His startled eyes slowly lose focus. He turns gray, then white. He drives and we watch the life seep out of him.

blackout.

music.

ext. outside motel. night.

'round the side of the motel, watched by a couple of cows, Yuri takes a piss against the wall. He climbs the steps and walks along the walkway to a blue door.

int. motel chalet 17. night.

Yuri enters the crusty motel suite. Alexei sits on a double bed counting the money.

Alexei says, "Ssshhh." He is counting in his head.

Nadia appears from the kitchenette area. They all seem more relaxed, more themselves, as if what we've seen before was an act.

> ALEXEI
>
> *(to Yuri)*
> *Ty pervy.*
> (Guess.)

> YURI
>
> *Pjatdesjat tysjach. Pochti v kopeechku.*
> (Twenty thousand.)

> NADIA
>
> *Shestdesjat chetyre tysjachi vosemsot.*
> (Twenty-four thousand, eight hundred.)

> ALEXEI
>
> *Zdes' bolshe chem vosemdesjat tysjach.*
> (There's over thirty grand here.)

They look at each other, absorbing the moment.

Alexei lies on top of the guitar cases and hugs them screaming: "Da! Da! Da!" He lies back on the bed and chuckles.

ALEXEI

Razlozhi vsjo po korobkam. Razdeli vsjo porovnu. I ne
zabud', chto ty mne dolzhen 150 funtov.
(Split it up three ways. And don't forget you owe me
150 pounds.)

YURI

Zachem escho?
(What for?)

ALEXEI

Sam znaesh' zacem.
(He's been flat broke since we got here.)

YURI

Ja tseluju nedelju tebe vsjo pokupal. Ja emu vsjo poku-
pal tseluju nedelju.
(I've been buying you stuff all week.)

ALEXEI

Chto ty mne pokupal?
(Such as?)

Nadia is smiling at them as they squabble.

YURI

Kogda my hodili v Hard Rock Cafe. Kto platil? Kogda
hodili smotret' Koshek. Kto platil?
(When we went to the Hard Rock Cafe. When we went
to see *Cats*. Who paid?)

ALEXEI

Eto ne nazyvaetsa padarkami. Eto normalnye veschi
mezdu druzjami.
(That's normal friendship stuff.)

They shout "Scmot" at each other.
    (Tightwad.)

Nadia interrupts them.

NADIA

Hey!
(pause)
Rasskazhi pro Koshek.
(What was *Cats* like?)

YURI

Normalno vsjo.
(It was all right.)

ALEXEI

Da vsjo bylo normalno.
(Yeah. It was so-so.)

YURI

*Na samom dele bylo dovolno klassno. Mne nekotorye
mesta dazhe ochen ponravilis'.*
(I'd give it three stars. Maybe three and a half.)

ALEXEI

Dekoratsii byli khoroshi.
(The sets were good.)

YURI

*Dekoratsii byli pervoklassyne. Vsjo bylo sdelano bol-
shim, ves' musor, vse butylki, bugami, musornye baki,
tak chto kogda smotrish', to kazhetsa chto ty sam
razmerom s kota. Vsjo bylo do melochei produmano.*
(The sets were excellent. Everything was big, you know,
all the rubbish, Coke cans, sweet wrappers, dustbins,
so when you were watching it you felt cat-size. It was
really clever.)

Yuri goes into the bathroom, leaving Nadia and Alexei alone. She sits on a chair beside the bed and smiles at him. He rolls onto his front, takes a swig of vodka, and wipes his mouth, watching her.

ALEXEI

(softly)
I chto. Skolko raz tebe prishlos's nim trakhatsa?
(So. How many times did you have to fuck him? Once? Twice?)

NADIA

You burned my head with the kettle.

cut to:

int. motel bathroom. night.

Yuri in the bathroom. He washes his hands in the sink. At the other end of the bathroom, tied to the bidet, gagged, is John.

YURI

How you doing? You okay?

John refuses to meet his eye. Yuri wipes his hands and squats beside him.

YURI (CONT'D)

Listen. Let me show you something. It should make all this easier, I think.

From his back pocket, Yuri removes a dozen or so Polaroids.

John looks down at the first Polaroid. Nadia, Alexei, and a man John doesn't recognize at a birthday party. There is a cake with candles and everyone is smiling. The next picture is the same. And the next.

YURI (CONT'D)

This is German guy. This is from Switzerland. This
is Greek . . . Greek guy. This is a croupier. This is fat
guy . . . and this is you.

*Sometimes Germany, sometimes France, but otherwise the pictures
are the same, each "fiancé" beaming with his arm 'round Nadia,
Alexei looking on. The final photo is of himself, taken that night in
his garden. We hear the guitar tune quietly reprise. Despite himself,
tears come to his eyes.*

*Yuri takes John's left hand and pulls off Nadia's ring. He puts it in his
pocket.*

int. motel bedroom. night.

*Alexei smokes on the bed. Nadia is lying the other way. She holds her
hand out for his cigarette and he passes it. They have the relaxed air
of longtime lovers.*

NADIA

Togo chto est' uzhe dostatochno, pravda?
(It's enough, isn't it?)

NADIA

*Ty znaesh' chto ja hochu skazat' mily. Uzhe dosatochno.
My mozhem ostanovitsa.*
(We can stop now.)

ALEXEI

Ty hochesh' ostanovitsa?
(Do you want to stop?)

NADIA

Da.
(Yes.)

ALEXEI

Horosho, togda ostanovimsa.
(We'll stop then.)

Pause. He takes her wrist, points at the marks there.

ALEXEI

A eto chto takoe?
(What's this?)

NADIA

Chto? Nichego. Obozhglas' prosto.
(I burned myself.)

ALEXEI

Sovsem na ozhog ne pokhozhe.
(A rope burn?)

NADIA

Skazala tebe. Gotovila obozhglas.
(I did it cooking.)

ALEXEI

Obi rouki?
(On both wrists?)

NADIA

Nu e chto? Gotovila e obozhglas'.
(What? I did it cooking.)

Alexei studies her face. She pulls a face. He keeps staring. Yuri pops out of the bathroom.

YURI

Ya v'passazh iduo. Ou nikh idzyot GranTurismo.
(I'm going over to the arcade. They've got
GranTurismo.)

75

He leaves.

Nadia gets up off the bed.

NADIA

Slushai, ya smasterila tsibyeh koe-chto.
(Listen, I made you something.)

She searches in her bag. Alexei watches her closely. She comes back up with the jumper she has knitted.

NADIA

Nadzyen.
(Put it on.)

He looks at the jumper, then back at her.

NADIA

Ya hochou ouvidzyets kak ohn sidzit.
(I want to see if it fits.)

She starts pulling at his shirt. Eventually he pulls the jumper on. It fits perfectly.

NADIA

Tsibyeh nravitsa?
(Do you like it?)

ALEXEI

Da.
(Yeah.)

NADIA

Nado skazat' spasibo.
(Say "thank you.")

ALEXEI

Spasibo.
(Thank you.)

He kisses her violently and they start making out passionately on the bed.

NADIA

Ou nas boudzyet ribyonok.
(We're going to have a baby.)

Alexei stops, holds her away.

ALEXEI

Chto?
(What?)

Nadia tries to hold him and kiss him again.

NADIA

Ty slyshal shto ya skazala. Ya beremenna.
(I'm pregnant. I've been throwing up for weeks.)

Alexei pushes her off him.

ALEXEI

A shto mui s'ribyonkom boudzyem dzyelats?
(What are we supposed to do with a baby?)

NADIA

Dadim emu imja.
(Think of a name for it.)

Pause.

Alexei stands up off the bed and casually walks into the bathroom.

int. motel bathroom. night.

John still sits tied to the bidet. Alexei walks in and closes the door. He stares ahead, as if John isn't there.

Presently Alexei pulls off the red sweater and leans over the sink, breathing deeply. He looks at himself in the mirror.

He exits, leaving John alone in the dark.

ext. john's close. night.

John's imaginings:

ext. john's close. night.

The cricket boys from John's close stand in a line in the middle of the street, bathed in flashing blue light. We pan 'round and end on John's house. It is surrounded with police. Police cars, police vans, plastic police tape "POLICE LINE. DO NOT CROSS." John's neighbors press against the tape: Clare, Robert Moseley, and the bank manager are all there in the crowd, as officers come and go.

cross-fade to:

int. motel. bathroom. night.

John's face, gagged, in the dark.

cross-fade to:

int. john's house. night.

Inside, the house is full of police, ransacking his possessions and dusting for fingerprints. A policeman is standing, reading The English-Russian dictionary.

int. john's house. landing. night.

We push on upstairs and along the landing to the spare room.

int. john's house. three locations. night.

An officer dumps a pile of porno magazines and videos on the bed. He then spots the belts tied to the bedstand and points them out to a detective. They exchange a knowing grin. A photographer steps up and snaps the paraphernalia in a blinding flash.

cross-fade to:

int. motel. bathroom. night.

John's face, gagged, in the dark.

cross-fade to:

The birthday cake is there, half-eaten. A policewoman puts it in a Baggie.

We pan across the bed, across the magazines and underwear in plastic bags, down below the bed, where we find the photograph of Nadia with the binoculars. The young girl smiles hopefully out at us from the past.

ext. dual carriageway. dawn.

Cars crawl by on the road outside, their taillights stretching into the distance. The early morning commuters now use the carriageway.

> RADIO ANNOUNCER (V/O)
> . . . and in St. Albans, an unnamed banker has stolen
> thirty thousand pounds from his own branch . . .

ext. motel walkway. day.

We push along to the blue door. Dissolve to:

int. motel. day.

The motel room is now empty. Dissolve to:

motel bathroom. day.

Bright sunlight pours through a high window. John is still on the toilet. He begins to try to struggle free.

After a great deal of fierce deadpan shimmying and pulling, he succeeds in loosening his bindings. Freeing an arm, he yanks the duct tape from his mouth and sits there panting.

The first thing he does is take a pee, then he drinks handfuls of water. He catches his reflection but can't look at himself.

int. motel bathroom. day.

John in the shower, just standing there, letting the water hit him.

int. motel main suite. day.

John dresses himself in silence. He painfully pulls on his shirt, and, one sock on, he walks to the smaller bedroom. He opens the door and peers inside.

int. smaller motel bedroom. day.

John enters the small bedroom. Tied to the radiator, gagged with duct tape, is Nadia.

John looks down at her. She looks at him. He walks out.

Close-up of Nadia's face. Her makeup is smudged and her eyes are full of tears. She watches him come back into the room and sit on the bed.

He watches her, then stands up, kneels by her, and starts untying her knots. He rips the tape off her mouth, painfully. He sits back on the bed. Suddenly he slaps her hard across the face.

Her head hits the radiator. Nadia gasps hard from the shock of the blow. She sits up and slaps him back, equally hard.

This starts a fight; kicking, hitting, biting, hairpulling, pinching; which takes them onto the bed. They wrestle here, then stop and look at each other: will they kiss? Suddenly, she kicks him off the bed and he lies there groaning. Slowly, he gets up, grabs the bedcover, and pulls it hard, rolling her off the bed. He falls back, landing in an armchair.

Nadia sits up from beside the bed and touches her bloody lip.

> NADIA (CONT'D)
> Great. You've split my fuckin' lip.

John stares at her. The blood pounds in his ears.

ext. dual carriageway. day.

The midmorning traffic flows by on the dual carriageway.

int. happy eater. day.

Nadia and John sit in silence in the half-empty diner. Nadia has a cut lip and a graze on her chin. John has a thousand-yard stare and a lesion over his left cheekbone.

A waitress approaches their table.

> WAITRESS
> Good morning. What can I get for you?

> NADIA
> I'll have an espresso with a small pastry or a croissant or . . .

> WAITRESS
> We only do a croissant with the continental breakfast.

> NADIA
> Just get me a coffee.

> WAITRESS
> And for you, sir?

John doesn't reply. He stares at Nadia.

NADIA

He'll have a coffee.

Pause.

NADIA

It's makes it easier. Okay.

Pause.

NADIA (CONT'D)

It makes it faster. I worked it out. If I don't speak
English the men, they fall faster.

*Nadia lights a cigarette and they sit in tense silence, the pain of
betrayal, and recent violence, thick in the air.*

NADIA

Why else would you send off for me? If you just wanted
sex, just go to a prostitute.

JOHN

Well, as it turns out, I did.

*She slaps his face. He slaps hers back. They wrestle over the table. The
waitress comes over.*

WAITRESS

Here you are.

JOHN

Lovely.

NADIA

I don't want it. Take it back.

JOHN

I'll have it. Lovely.

She puts it in front of John.

WAITRESS

Pleasure.

JOHN

(to the waitress)
Oh, excuse me . . . do you know where the nearest
police station is?

WAITRESS

Uh . . . that would be Radlett. It's two junctions
in . . . that direction. One or two, I can't
remember.

JOHN

About five, ten minutes . . . ?

WAITRESS

Five or ten. It's not far.

JOHN

Lovely. Perfect. Thanks.

WAITRESS

Pleasure.

She smiles and leaves them. John watches her walk away.

NADIA

John, I need your help.

He laughs so much he has to put his coffee down.

84

JOHN

You must think. I'm the biggest pillock.
In the world.

NADIA

I know you just want to punish me . . .

JOHN

I do. I want to very badly.

NADIA

So you're just going to be vindictive.

JOHN

In every sense. If at all possible.

NADIA

You can't hurt me more than I'm hurt already.

JOHN

Well, Nadia, if it's all the same to you, I'd like to give it a
bash.

Pause.

NADIA

My name is not Nadia.

John stares back at her.

int. police station duty desk. day.

*They sit side by side in the waiting room, not talking. Nadia looks
resigned to her fate. John is tight-jawed, unyielding. He removes
his tie from his pocket and puts it on. He flattens his hair.*

85

They wait as the duty sergeant deals with a woman who has lost her hat.

NADIA

(quietly to John)
Where's the toilet?

JOHN

What?

NADIA

I'm going to be sick. Where's the . . .

JOHN

What? No, you're not..

NADIA

I'm going . . . I am . . . I'm going to be sick.

JOHN

(OVERLAPPING)

No, you're not. How . . . Nice one. How stupid do you think I am?

Nadia stands and addresses the duty sergeant.

NADIA

Where's the restroom?

SERGEANT

The what, love?

NADIA

The toilet. Where's—

SERGEANT

Through that door, up the stairs and it's on the left.

She heads off. John springs up. He seizes her arm as casually as possible.

int. police station corridor. day.

John frogmarches Nadia down the corridor to the ladies'. She wrestles her arm free again and disappears inside.

John lurks outside. He seems certain she's got one leg out the window RIGHT NOW.

He can't bear it any longer. He looks both ways and nips inside.

int. ladies'. day.

Standing in the Ladies, John hears Nadia in a cubicle, throwing up. He hears the toilet flush.

Nadia comes out. He looks at her.

JOHN

You're pregnant.

Nadia looks at the floor.

int. police corridor. day.

John walks out of the toilet and stands against the wall of the corridor. He looks both ways. After a few seconds, Nadia appears in the corridor. They stand there. John isn't looking at her.

A policeman appears from 'round the corner, and walks toward them.
He stops and addresses John.

>   POLICEMAN
> Can I help you?

John looks at the policeman, then at Nadia. The seconds pass.

>   POLICEMAN
> Sir? Can I help you?

John is still looking at Nadia. He closes his eyes.

>   JOHN
> No. Thank you.

ext. outside police station. day.

John walks back to the Capri, Nadia behind. They reach the
car.

int. police station. day.

A fax comes through a fax machine: a blurred image of John's
face.

>   POLICEMAN (V/O)
> Yeah, name of suspect: John Buckingham. Believed
> sighted today approx eleven twenty-one hours, Radlett
> Constabulary. Ref. one zero seven foxtrot alpha.

A policeman takes the fax, looks at it, and pins it to a noticeboard.

ext. motorway. day.

John's car pulls onto the motorway. From a bridge we watch it drive away.

> RADIO ANNOUNCER (V/O)
> A St. Albans bank clerk is on the run today after stealing £32,000 in broad daylight from his own branch. John Buckingham, who lived alone and had been with the branch for ten years, was described by bosses as a workhorse.

int/ext. moving car. day.

John drives. Nadia looks out of the window. The radio is on.

> RADIO ANNOUNCER (V/O) (CONT'D)
> Now police are on the lookout for a bright orange MGB GT, registration AGV 932Y.

> JOHN
> *(flatly)*
> Have you got your passport?

> RADIO ANNOUNCER (V/O) (CONT'D)
> Several colleagues expressed shock at the daring of the raid, carried out shortly after . . .

ext. motorway junction.

From above we watch the car turn off the motorway, around a roundabout, and into a country B road.

cross-fade to:

Images of the bank colleagues pass across the screen.

BRANCH MANAGER

John's been with us for ten years, and I think I speak for us all when I say I hope he gets ten years.

MOSELEY

Banking asks a great deal of an individual. It says: Here's all this money, don't steal it.

CLARE

I mean, we are insured for this sort of thing so it's not the money. It's just, I sat next to him for years and he seemed perfectly normal.

cross-fade to:

ext. country lane. day.

John's car shimmering as it comes over the brow of a remote country lane, surrounded by fields and rolling hills.

int/ext. car (moving). day.

They are driving along.

NADIA

I want you to know I appreciate this. And I'm sorry that you are a fugitive from justice.

JOHN

I'd find this a whole lot easier if you don't talk, at all, for the rest of the day.

NADIA

John, in Russia there's no work for women.

JOHN

And here we go . . .

NADIA

What?

JOHN

No, go on. I've actually been looking forward to this bit.

NADIA

What?

JOHN

"In Russia it is so bad, we have to eat each other in the winter. We have to go to England and shag men just to keep warm."

NADIA

I'm just saying, for women there, life is very hard.

JOHN

And you thought you'd take that out on me.

NADIA

The rest of the world is not all like St. Albans.

JOHN

Well, thank Christ for that.
So, how do you do it?

NADIA

We put a picture on the Web sites, find men who work in finance . . .

JOHN

No. No. I mean how do you do it with men you hate?

NADIA

I don't hate you.

JOHN

Right. So, Alexei. Not the kids type then?

NADIA

He will be back.

JOHN

Excuse me?

NADIA

He left me my ticket and passport. So it's pretty clear he wants to see me again.

JOHN

Yeah. Actually, I tend to tie up and abandon women I really want to see again, too.

NADIA

No. But you tie them up.

John freezes. Nadia watches him.

NADIA (CONT'D)
Oh, so you don't want to talk about *that.*

John stares ahead.

NADIA (CONT'D)
Okay, we won't talk about it. We'll say it never happened.

JOHN

Okay. Okay. When you were a little girl running around with your binoculars, did you think, "When I grow up I

92

want to fuck loads of strange men, steal their homes, jobs and dignity. But what I really want is to end up on my own, up the duff, flat broke, on a plane back to the boonies?

NADIA

So tell me, John, when you were a schoolboy in St. Albans, did you say, "When I grow up, what I want is to still be in this town, in this job I hate, a house full of ants, and a big bag of pornography. Then I'm going to send off for a wife from Russia and she'll fall in love with me"? What did you expect, John? What did you really expect to happen?

JOHN

You don't know me.

NADIA

And you don't know me either.

John pulls the car over sharply.

JOHN

Get out.

NADIA

You are throwing me out.

JOHN

Get out.

She collects her bag from the backseat, her cigarettes, gathers up her belongings, clicks open the door, and gets out, leaving the shot.

NADIA

You prefer your women mute.

John turns the key in the ignition. The engine bellows and screams. Silence.

He tries again. The engine shrieks and wails like a soul in torment. A terrible, mournful grinding noise. Silence.

John tries to start it. It lets out a whimper, a crying, a few shuddering, moving sobs, and dies.

Nadia pokes her head through the window.

NADIA

Car trouble?

John sits in his dead car. He shakes his head. He rubs his face. He sits there.

int. car on deserted country road. day.

Fifteen minutes later. Now Nadia sits alone in the dead car. John sits about thirty feet in front of the car, on the grass, staring across the fields. Nadia honks the horn. She leans out of the window.

NADIA

Hey. They are looking for this car, John. This is not a very good plan.

John doesn't react. She reaches over and opens the glove box and finds a Milky Way. She rips it open and takes a bite, watching John. She looks back at the glove box. There is a folded bank slip with Nadia written on it. She opens it.

It is a note, written in bad Russian. As we hear her reading it, we see the translation, in subtitles:

SUBTITLE

Dear Nadia, I like you. You are only girl in the world.
I dream to talk. What will happen? John.

*Nadia looks at John over the dashboard, sitting on the grass. She
looks guilty, and sad, and alone.*

ext. country road. day.

*John and Nadia push the orange car off the road and down a slope
where it rolls faster and faster until it crashes into a tree hidden in
the woods.*

ext. the forest. dusk.

*John and Nadia walk through the woods. We follow John's
face.*

ext. the forest. night.

*In a clearing, John watches Nadia carry a pile of sticks to a fire
she is building. She lights it with her gun cigarette lighter, and
teases the flames to life.*

int. hotel room. night.

*Alexei is packing his suitcase on the bed. He is putting complimentary
toiletries into his case.*

int. hotel bathroom. night.

Yuri lies in the bath reading aloud from a Spanish travel brochure. "Memory" from Cats plays in the background.

int. hotel room. night.

Alexei finds the jumper she knitted. He smells it.

He holds it up and looks at it. He glances down, and spots something that has fallen out of it, something that stops him dead.

A tiny baby jumper has fallen onto the floor. It is identical to his, but tiny.

Alexei sits on the bed, holding the jumper and staring at it.

ext. forest. night.

John and Nadia sit by the fire. She smokes.

A fox cries out in the night.

> NADIA
> Listen. I think it's a fox.

She listens. It cries out again. She gets out her binoculars.

> NADIA (CONT'D)
> I can't see anything. It's too dark.

She looks through them and searches the brush. John watches Nadia with her binoculars. He looks suddenly very sad.

> NADIA
> What happened between you and the blonde?

JOHN

What?

NADIA

The thin . . . the girl with small eyes. The one in your
cupboard.

JOHN

It's none of your business. She didn't have small
eyes.

NADIA

Did she leave you? Come on. It's nothing to be
ashamed of. Who did she leave you for? Your best
friend? Her boss? A woman? Did she leave you for
a woman ,John?

JOHN

She's dead.

Pause.

NADIA

I'm sorry. I didn't mean to hurt you.

Pause.

NADIA (CONT'D)

Forgive me.

JOHN

I don't know why I said that. She's not dead
at all.

Nadia looks at John.

NADIA

What?

JOHN

I don't know why I said it. I'm sorry.

NADIA

She's alive?

Nadia starts to laugh. Long and loud. We have never seen her laugh before.

NADIA (CONT'D)

She is not dead?

JOHN

Laugh it up.

She starts to cough. She gets on her hands and knees and coughs like fury.

JOHN (CONT'D)

You should stop smoking. You're pregnant.
You smoke like a bastard.

NADIA

I'm trying to quit.

JOHN

It's not working.

NADIA

I smoke more when I'm unhappy.

JOHN

Nobody's that unhappy.

NADIA

Maybe I want to die. Don't you want me to die?

JOHN

I don't want anyone to die.

NADIA

Except for Small Eyes.

JOHN

Except for Small Eyes.

She laughs again.

NADIA

So why did it end?

John thinks. It looks as if he's going to tell the whole story. In the end he shrugs.

JOHN

I don't know.

NADIA

What was her name?

JOHN

What's your name?

They listen to the fox crying in the night.

Nadia curls up on the other side of the fire, and hugs herself.

John lies, staring at the stars.

Music.

ext. countryside. day.

We dissolve between three five-second shots of the pair walking at different times of the day.

ext. field. day.

A shimmering late sun. We find John and Nadia coming toward us through the late heat haze.

They aren't speaking and both look tired. As they pass we crane up out of the corn to catch an enormous 757 Jumbo Jet just above us, coming in to land. We pan 'round to see, half a mile away, the massive airport beyond.

They walk toward it, two tiny figures.

cut to:

int. airport. dusk.

We see the departures board with the Moscow flight listed.

int. airport. dusk.

An attendant pushes a train of trolleys past. Businessmen talk into mobile phones.

NADIA

> I've got some time. Can I buy you a
> coffee?

JOHN

No. I think I better just go.

Nadia hesitates. There's just a hint of regret in this good-bye.

NADIA

This is for you.

She hands him a package, wrapped up.

JOHN

Yeah. No thanks.

NADIA

Please. Why not?

John shrugs. He takes it.

NADIA

Good-bye.

John nods and turns.

int/ext. airport exit. dusk.

John walks away, and Nadia goes out of focus and becomes a blur. We Steadicam close to John's face until he has left the airport. We pull back to find him standing on the concourse.

Waiting, John opens his package. It's the binoculars. He turns them over in his hands.

int. airport. dusk.

POV through the binoculars. Passengers crisscross, but we find Nadia sitting alone, waiting for her call.

John lowers the binoculars and gazes across the airport. He raises them for one last look.

Nadia, glimpsed through the crowd. We spy someone approaching about twenty feet behind her. It is ALEXEI.

John lowers the binoculars, horrified. He looks again.

We watch Alexei approach her. She looks up and is completely thrown. Yuri stands about ten feet away, shifty in shades, checking his watch.

Nadia pulls her arm away. Alexei crouches down in front of her and puts a hand on her knee, coaxing her.

Alexei takes her by the arm and leads her away.

int. airport. night.

John hurries into the airport. They are walking toward him. He steps back into the crowd and they pass in front of him, heading for the lift. He follows them, racing down the elevator and to the exit.

ext. airport. night.

John watches them get into a taxi and hears Yuri speak to the driver.

YURI
The Skye Grand Hotel, across the way.

The taxi pulls off.

102

John runs across the approach road toward the car park and over a low fence.

ext. slip road to airport. night.

John reaches the road just as the taxi passes. He ducks out of view then runs after it.

ext. grassy verge. night.

John runs after the cab. We crane up to see the cab heading for the airport hotel.

ext. roundabout. night.

The cab pulls away from the hotel. We follow it away to see John running up behind it. He heads for the hotel.

int. hotel foyer. night.

John rushes into the foyer. He can't see them anywhere. He approaches the front desk.

> JOHN
>
> Two Russians just came past, with a woman.
> Which room are they in?

> CONCIERGE
>
> I'm sorry, sir, I'm afraid we can't give out room
> numbers.

> JOHN
>
> She left something in my cab.

John takes the binoculars out of his pocket.

                    CONCIERGE
          We'll make sure she gets them.

He takes the binoculars from John and walks away.

A porter arrives behind the desk, carrying a large, framed photograph of the concierge, which he hangs on the wall.

                    JOHN
          Excuse me. Two Russians are staying here. Do you
          know which floor they're on?

                    PORTER
          Yes, I know which floor they're on.

John pulls a banknote out of his pocket and slides it across the desk.

                    JOHN
          And which floor would that be?

                    PORTER
          We've only got one floor.

The porter pockets the banknote and walks off.

                    JOHN
          Thanks.

The Concierge returns and stares at John, who leaves.

ext. hotel perimeter. night.

John skirts around the edge of the hotel. He peers in through one of the windows.

ext. back of hotel. night.

At the back of the hotel he looks through another couple of windows.

ext./int. view through the window. night.

John can see a young businessman in shirt and pants, sitting on the bed, talking on the phone.

ext. back of hotel. night.

John checks a couple more. Suddenly he drops like he's been shot.

Warily he looks again.

ext./int. the view through the window.

Inside, Yuri is packing the money into black bin-liners and putting them in large pockets inside Alexei's coat.

ext. back of hotel. night.

John scampers to the next window and looks inside.

ext./int. the view through the window.

Alexei kneels opposite Nadia, who sits on a chair. She is avoiding his eye as he appeals. Before long she looks at him.

Alexei tries to kiss her. She turns her face. He tries again, and she pushes him away. Finally, she accepts the kiss. Her resolve seems to melt and she kisses him back.

ext. outside alexei's suite. night.

John stares through the window at the scene.

int. inside alexei's suite. night.

Back in the room, Yuri pops his head 'round the door and says something to Alexei. Alexei says he's coming. He kisses Nadia again and leaves.

Nadia is alone.

ext. outside alexei's suite. night.

John's face at the window.

ext. outside alexei's suite. night.

John watches Nadia rush over to the wardrobe and searches for something. She gets on her hands and knees and looks under the bed.

Behind her, Alexei reappears in the doorway. He watches her looking under the bed. She sits up and sees him.

Alexei walks into the room holding his coat. He indicates: Is this what you were looking for?

He throws the coat on the floor in front of her and shouts, pushing her.

There is a knock at the door. Alexei answers. A porter, Tim, hands him the binoculars, which he accepts, shutting the door and putting them on the dressing table. Close-up of Nadia's face, staring at them.

Alexei seizes her, hits her with a parcel of the money, and pushes her onto the bed.

ext. outside alexei's suite. night.

John outside.

> JOHN
>
> Oh, Jesus.

John ducks down, panting, swallowing hard. At once he springs up and skirts the building again. With real effort he pries the next window open—it is a bathroom. He pulls himself up and drops inside.

int. alexei's bathroom/hallway. night.

John lands in the bathroom and scampers across the floor. He opens the bathroom door a crack. He is at the opposite end of a corridor from the bedroom. He can hear Alexei's voice.

Breathing hard, he tiptoes out and stands in the corridor, his back pressed hard against the wall. He takes one step down the hall. The floor creaks loudly.

int. alexei's suite hallway. night.

John takes another step down the hallway. We hear Alexei and Nadia shouting at each other.

John notices Nadia's bag by the door.

Crouching, he opens the bag and searches inside. He finds what he is looking for: the silver pistol cigarette lighter.

John is absolutely terrified, breathing hard and shaking, holding the little "gun." Next door the row has subsided.

int. alexei's suite. night.

The door bursts open.

Alexei turns to see John standing by the door, holding a little silver gun.

NADIA

What are you doing?

John and Nadia look at each other.

ALEXEI

Kakogo chorta emu zdes nado?
(What the fuck is he doing here?)

He looks at the little gun.

ALEXEI (CONT'D)

Eto ved' ta samaja zazhigalka, chto ja tebe podaril?
(That's that cigarette lighter I gave you, isn't it?)

Alexei stands. John takes a step back. Alexei walks calmly toward John, takes the lighter, and throws a punch. It catches John right on the chin and he hits the wall and goes down very fast.

NADIA

Ostanovis'!
(Leave him!)

Alexei turns to look at his lover, confused and then angry.

>ALEXEI
>
>*Tui shto? Za nivo?*
>(What? Are you on his side?)

>NADIA
>
>*Ostav evo v pokoe!*
>(He came here with me!)

>ALEXEI
>
>*Yawb tvoyaw . . . tui vlyoubilas, v'etovov moudakah.*
>(You mean . . . you're together?)

Alexei turns and kicks John in the head.

>NADIA
>
>*Nichevo ya ne vlyubilas.*
>(No. It's not what you think.)

Suddenly he snatches up the knife and stands above her.
Shouting in Russian, he forces John and Nadia onto the bed.

>ALEXEI
>
>*Nou davai. Yesli tui yevo lyoubish, davai posmotrim,*
>*kak ty yevo trakhayesh. Davai, poshla.*
>(Come on then. Let's see how much you love him.)

>NADIA
>
>*Njet.*
>(No.)

>ALEXEI
>
>*Davai, poshla. Ja hochu posmotret' kak tui*
>*boudzyesh tselovats etoh dzyermo. Davai tselui.*
>(Do it. I want to see how you do it. Kiss him.)

NADIA

Njet.
(No.)

JOHN

What's he's saying?

NADIA

Nothing.

JOHN

What's he saying? Tell me.

Alexei is pushing John onto Nadia. He has the knife at John's neck.

NADIA

Ostav menja v pokoe . . .
(Don't do this . . .)

ALEXEI

Pokazhi mne. Ne budesh tselovat ja ego ubju. Ty znaesh, chto ja eto sdelaju.
(Show me. I'll make a big mess here.)

He pushes the knife to John's neck.

Nadia looks at Alexei. She looks at John, and she kisses him.

The sound on the film goes silent. They kiss for ten seconds. John's eyes remain open. When she stops, John is looking at her, but she can't look at him. John has tears in his eyes.

The sound returns as Alexei slumps down against the wardrobe, holding his head. He is in anguish. He drops the knife, shaking. Suddenly he throws himself at the bed like an animal.

He hurls John out of the way—he flies across the room and crashes onto the floor. Alexei lands on her and, tears rolling down his face, begins throttling her. It is as if he is preparing to rape her, when John smashes the edge of the guitar down on the back of his head. It emits a final fruity chord.

cut to:

alexei's suite. night.

Nadia stands at the window and stares at her reflection, or past it into the blackness.

Alexei is tied to a chair, staring at her imploringly. He speaks.

SUBTITLE
Don't leave me here. At least leave my share.

She firmly places a piece of duct tape over his mouth. We see a hand remove Alexei's ticket and passport from his jacket.

NADIA
Your money's in his coat. In the lining.

John picks up the coat. It's heavy. They leave. Alexei hops to the door on his chair, protesting numbly.

int. airport checking-in desk. night.

John carries the coat full of money. Nadia just has her small camouflaged carryall. They race through the airport, and come to a stop at the ramp that leads to the departure gates.

111

                    JOHN

      Are you okay?

She nods.

                    JOHN

      Okay. Good-bye.

                    NADIA

      Good-bye.

They shake.

                    JOHN

      What're you going to do?

Nadia shrugs.

                    NADIA

      I don't know. Something else . . .

                    JOHN

      Promise?

                    NADIA

      Promise.

They stand around.

                    NADIA (CONT'D)

      Good-bye.

                    JOHN

      Good-bye.

She leans forward and kisses him.

As they kiss, John puts the coat 'round her shoulders.

Nadia breaks the kiss and looks at him.

> NADIA
>
> This isn't mine.

> JOHN
>
> It's not mine either.

> NADIA
>
> I don't want it. I can't take it.

> JOHN
>
> You could spend it on the baby.

She leans forward and whispers in his ear. John looks at her. He looks to the four corners of the airport. And back at her.

> JOHN
>
> Why?

> NADIA
>
> I'm not asking you to marry me.

> JOHN
>
> It's a long way to go for a date.

> NADIA
>
> I know.

> JOHN
>
> But . . . I don't know you.

> NADIA
>
> And I don't know you either.

Pause.

int. hotel corridor/alexei's suite. night.

Whistling, Yuri comes out of his suite, knocks briskly on the door of Alexei's, and enters. We walk with him down the hallway into the bedroom to find an empty chair, surrounded by ropes.

Yuri murmurs something in Russian.

SUBTITLE

Fuck a duck.

ext. airport hotel. night.

Alexei jumps into the back of a cab and shouts at the driver in Russian.

int. airport boarding gate. flight 1311 to moscow. night.

John and Nadia approach the X-ray machines and join parallel queues John takes the leather coat and puts it on. She whispers in his ear.

NADIA

Just say yes, just say *da* . . .

John pushes Alexei's passport and ticket under the Perspex window and looks at the young airport official, the blood beating in his ears.

Nadia begins talking to him in Russian. Each time she pauses, John just says da. She checks through passport control.

For a few interminable seconds the official's eyes burn into John.

CLOSE SHOT: *The passport is snapped shut and pushed back through.*

cut to:

int. airport. night.

Alexei races into the aiport, feeling in his inside pocket. He comes to a stop. His ticket and passport aren't there.

int. airport boarding gate. flight 1311 to moscow. night.

John walks on to the metal detector. He is about to pass through when he stops. He reaches into his pocket, takes out the binoculars and places them in the dish. He steps through, retrieves them and walks on.

int. airport boarding corridor. night.

The two of them round a corner and walk briskly towards us.

NADIA

My name's Sophia.

JOHN

Sophia.
Hello, Sophia. Mine's still John.

SOPHIA

Hello, John.

They walk side by side without speaking, onto a travelator.

*They stop walking and float along, both looking forward,
straight-faced. John looks across at Nadia and she glances back.
They smile.*

They float toward us and disappear.

SFX. The roar of jet engines.

ext. airport runway. sunset.

*With a deafening roar an Aeroflot Boeing 757 lifts slowly from
the runway and climbs up into the night sky, where it becomes a
distant star.*

ext. field. day.

A distant airplane in a cobalt blue sky, through binoculars.

*The young girl from the very first scene lowers the binoculars and
lets them hang around her neck. She squints up at the sun.*

A voice calls her.

> WOMAN'S VOICE
> Nadia!

The girl looks round.

> WOMAN'S VOICE
> Nadia!

*She runs past us and we track her to her mother sitting on a
blanket on the ground. It's Sophia. John is there, holding a birthday
cake, candles aflame. He sets it down on the blanket. The little girl,*

Nadia, blows out her candles and we helicopter up as the guitar theme plays.

The family gets smaller and smaller as the huge Russian landscape beyond grows and grows, as far as the eye can see.

THE END